Sophie Corrigan

PUGTATO

babysits the snouts

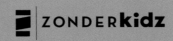

ZONDERkidz

Pugtato was busy doing his chores in the garden

when the Brussels snouts' parents said, "We do beg your pardon!

We're off to the market, would
you please watch the snouts?
They've asked just for you.
It would really help us out!"

Pugtato said,
"No problem,
I'll do my best!"

Though the snouts were a handful,
he didn't protest.

"I'll carry you babies.
Each one gets a turn."

Then the three little snouts who were eager to play,
carried big ole' Pugtato the rest of the way.

As they passed Seedling Square
and a group of cute daisies

the Brussels snouts sang,
"Don't forget—we're *NOT* babies!"

Inside the nursery it was busy and bright,
Pugtato just knew to keep those snouts in his sight!

The artichicks painted pots up on a shelf.
That's safe for babies! Pugtato thought to himself.

So he passed around brushes
and small pots of paint
and the three snouts hopped to it
without a complaint!

So the group found some
sequins, pom-poms, and glue,
then spruced up the plants,
and Pugtato's face too!

Pugtato woofed with joy as bell pupper skipped by.

"Look babies, jump twine!
Let's all give that a try!"

"Dear spud,
we're NOT babies,
we're all quite grown up!"

Then the Brussels snouts showed their skills to the pup.

They teetered and tottered along the tightrope-twine,
but with the snout's help, their spuddy
cycled just fine!

His round 'tato body helped them balance with ease,

and they wound up near some
splashing baby croccolis!

Soon a bucket was filled and the group all jumped in, apart from Pugtato, who just couldn't swim.

While he wanted to jump in the pool with the snouts, he said, "My trunks are at home, so I'll sit this one out."

"Don't be a BABY!" the snouts said. "Hold steady ...
Ok then, Pugtato ... NOW you are ready!"

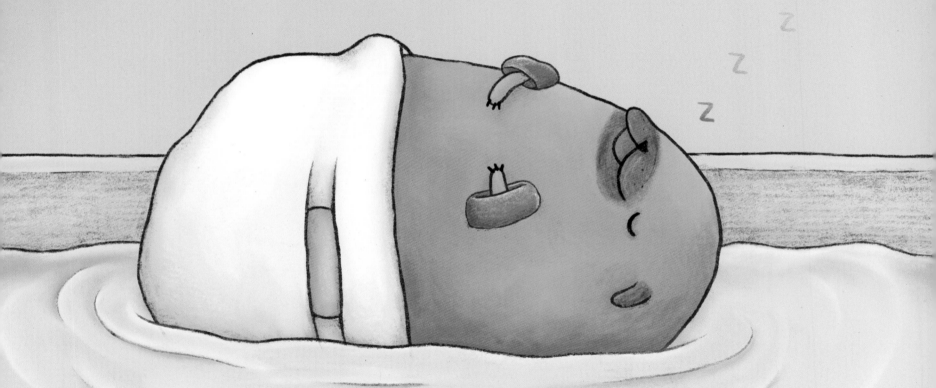

"Well, this is lovely! Babysitting's a breeze.
Today has gone well and I've done it with ease."

He closed his eyes, smiling as he floated about ...

But suddenly thought,

WHERE ARE THE SNOUTS?!

"Oh no!" woofed Pugtato, as he felt his eyes widen,
and he threw off his floaties and
jumped out to find them.

Pugtato declared, "I will come and get you!"
And he climbed up the rocks to perform a rescue.

But they wobbled and
wiggled and started to fall.

"Perhaps babysitting's
NOT my thing after all."

As Pugtato was falling,
his head full of doubt,

He was caught in mid-air
by the hoof of a snout!

They giggled and sang as they swung plant to plant,

"See, we're NOT babies!" was the Brussels snouts' chant.

They landed outside in a big
veggie pile and said,

"That's the most fun
we've had in a while!"

Pugtato was tired from his long day of play,
and he fell fast asleep as the snouts led the way.

"It's time for our spuddy
to rest his sweet head."

And they plopped their friend down
on the soft flower bed.

When the snouts saw their parents,
they gave them a hug,
as Pugtato lay sleeping
all snug as a bug.

"Of course you can ...
but I'm
NOT
a BABY!"

ZONDERKIDZ

Pugtato Babysits the Snouts
Copyright © 2021 by Sophie Corrigan
Illustrations © 2021 by Sophie Corrigan

Requests for information
should be addressed to:

Zonderkidz, 3900 Sparks Dr. SE,
Grand Rapids, Michigan 49546

Hardcover ISBN 978-0-310-73411-6

Ebook ISBN 978-0-310-73412-3

Design: Diane Mielke

Printed in South Korea

21 22 23 24 25 26 /SAM/ 13 12 11 10 9 8 7 6 5 4 3 2 1